to Tame a Gambler

Nancy Pirri

Fortune, goodnight. Smile once more; turn thy wheel.

WILLIAM SHAKESPEARE

one

September 1880
Bozeman, Montana

The woman had her nose stuck in a Bible from the time John O'Connell boarded the stagecoach twenty miles south of Bozeman. He envied her position. She had been lucky in securing a corner seat beside a window, with only one person on the side of her. He was squeezed between two decidedly plump matrons wearing fake-fruit decorated bonnets and reeking of lavender water. Damned lucky he wasn't any bigger or the three of them wouldn't fit.

"Bozeman's right up yonder!" the driver called out cheerily over the thundering of the horses' hooves.

John dusted off his black pants and jacket, in the process jabbing both women with his elbows. They glared at him.

"Sorry," he apologized. "I think we are all more than ready to get out into the fresh air."

"Amen," said the woman on his left, giving him a near toothless grin.

John shifted his gaze to the woman across from him, trying to estimate her age. Upon settling inside the coach, he saw her face in profile. She appeared young. Then, sitting across from her, she had raised her Bible and had not lowered it—not once. Between the book concealing her face and the small veiled felt hat on her head, he had no idea what she looked like. Her traveling attire was appropriate. She wore a brown woolen jacket and skirt with velvet collar and cuffs.

He breathed a relieved sigh when he glanced out the window and saw people walking the streets, coaches being pulled by horses, buggies rumbling by. Ah, the sounds of city life—exciting and exotic!—the noise of people living life to the fullest. He couldn't wait to leave the coach and set foot on solid ground.

They'd reached the Bozeman Coach Station. The coach door opened, and the driver set down a set of rickety wooden stairs, then leaned in to help the first woman out. "Lord, it'll be wonderful to stretch our legs a bit, won't it?" she said.

John nodded. "You are correct, madam."

He pulled himself easily out of the coach after the woman, then turned and helped the woman who'd been on his right. She gave him a simpering smile. He sighed, mindful of the fact that women—young and old—were attracted to him. He was handsome enough, he supposed, but it wasn't his looks that attracted them, it was his polite, respectful manners, instilled in him by his gentle mama. Though, when angry, that tiny woman wielded a switch better than a two-hundred-pound man.

The last person he assisted from the carriage was the bookish gal. She accepted his hand as she made her way down the steps, then quickly dropped it with a murmured, "Thank you," once her feet touched the ground. John felt his heart quicken when he got his first good look at the pretty young woman who stood no taller than his shoulder.

She took a step, stumbled and dropped her Bible.

He reached out a quick hand, cupped her elbow to steady her then released her when he was certain she was steady on her feet. When he bent to pick up the book, she did, too, and they bumped heads. Rubbing his forehead, he murmured, "Sorry, miss. Just trying to be help..." pausing when he looked at the Bible and saw another book tucked inside. A small one, its pages bent and ragged.

Still crouched, he glanced at the Bible's owner who bent down facing him. Looking at her, John felt as though he'd been struck by lightning. He was drawn to the clear-eyed sign of intelligence in her eyes behind a pair of gold-rimmed metal spectacles. He glimpsed, beneath her bonnet, rich auburn-colored hair.

He reached for the book. She did too, and her hand landed on top of his. She tried pulling the book from his hand, but he kept a grip on it, curious to know what she'd been hiding in the Bible.

Tearing his gaze away from her pleading expression, he glanced down and closed the smaller book to reveal the cover. *Murder and Love in Tucson City.* She'd concealed a trashy dime store novel between the pages of her Bible. She wouldn't meet his eyes, just held out her hand.

He gave her the book. Without a word, she tucked it back inside the Bible. Staring at her a moment longer, he saw she wore a veiled hat that came down over her eyes. Beneath the veil, her nose was small and slightly pointy.

They rose simultaneously. He said, "Madam? I'm curious about—"

She murmured, "Please, don't ask." Her soft, gentle southern drawl intrigued him.

He'd met several southern belles since the Civil War

years, and all of them were pleasant and well-mannered, not to mention undeniably feminine.

It was disappointing that she had been reading a 'penny dreadful.' He'd read a few himself to see what all the fuss was about. In his opinion, they equaled trash— unmitigated trash. Why would a perfectly respectable woman read such an unsavory book?

She walked quickly away from him to the stagecoach station. Striding after her, he said, "Madam? May I assist you to your lodgings?"

She raised one finely shaped eyebrow and glanced at him over her shoulder, her foot on the first step. "No, thank you. I can manage."

"I insist on accompanying you. Where are you staying?"

"At the St. Angel's Home for Women," she muttered.

The coachman brought over her bags, taking three trips to do so. "Think that's everything," he said before stalking away, kicking up dust in his wake.

John looked down and sighed. The woman had packed three enormous valises. "Excuse me a moment."

He entered the station building and, for a few dollars, found a boy willing to haul their luggage and them in a wagon to St. Angel's. Good Lord, John hoped the place wasn't a nunnery. Then he thought about her choice of reading material and decided it was highly unlikely.

He stepped back outside and their gazes collided, hers direct and intent.

Her brown eyes didn't appear a bit myopic, which made him think she didn't require spectacles. Frowning, he wondered why a pretty woman would conceal her eyes behind a pair of spectacles if she didn't need to. She was an enigma.

"I'm John O'Connell."

"Grace Morgan," she murmured.

John bowed, taking her small, gloved hand in his. "Glad to make your acquaintance, Miss Morgan."

She smiled back. John noted how it didn't quite reach her eyes.

"I'm new in town. How about you?"

She gave him a brilliant smile. "Oh, yes, quite new."

He nearly gasped aloud at her beauty. "Will you be staying long?"

"I'm...I'm not sure yet." She added, "I'd like to leave for St. Angel's, if you don't mind. I'm exhausted."

"Of course you are," he said and solicitously took her arm.

The boy came around from the back, driving a buckboard loaded with their bags. He jumped down, leaving John to drive.

John assisted Miss Morgan into her seat. When he climbed up beside her, she brushed her skirts out of his way. He sank against the back of the seat and enjoyed the soft brush of her arm against his. She looked away and he took the opportunity to peruse her once more. When he raised his gaze, he found her staring at him. Her lips formed into a little smile, and her eyes sparkled with humor.

"You, I believe, are no gentleman, sir," she said softly.

He grinned. "There's no crime in looking, is there? Besides, I'd be less than human to ignore a pretty woman."

She shrugged. "I suppose there isn't, though I believe I read more than mere admiration in your eyes."

"No chance of that. I've been accused of having the best poker face around."

"Did you say—poker?"

He nodded.

"Are you, perhaps, a gambling man, Mr. O'Connell?"

John's smile widened. "No. I'm a teacher."

Grace breathed a relieved sigh. A teacher—not a gambler. Good. One less person with whom to compete. She'd heard of the tough competition in the gambling establishments across the west before setting out from her home in Atlanta, Georgia. She considered herself just as tough. Not only had it been said that *she* possessed the best 'poker face' around, but she also usually won every hand she played. A seasoned player, she'd not only acquired the skill but had been blessed with amazing good luck. Gambling was her legacy from her father.

She earned her living by gambling, but her passion was writing, not penny dreadfuls, by choice, however. She'd written two full-length novels but had yet to find a publisher. The penny dreadfuls, while not as popular as they were in the past several years, were snatched up by a publisher, though, and as long as she could keep handing over a chapter a week to print, she'd keep the relationship. Until her novels sold. And while she had written and published three penny dreadfuls thus far, writing had proven not to be as lucrative an endeavor as gambling.

Grace thought about how Mr. O'Connell had found her reading the penny dreadful. The book was one of the better ones she'd read of late. It was important she keep abreast of her competition. She didn't like that John had discovered her secret. Curiosity had stolen across his face. Thankfully, she'd been able to squelch his questions.

His arm brushed against her and she glanced up at him before turning to the view once more. John O'Connell was big, rugged, and handsome, and seemed to be oblivious of the fact. A nice trait, she decided as she thought about some of her past beaus. They had possessed an unbearably annoying amount of narcissism, which was not a bit to her liking.

Pulling her wayward thoughts away from the handsome gentleman at her side, she took great delight in the sights and scents of Bozeman as the buggy swept past buildings painted in bright swathes of color. Shops galore lined the streets. It had been a long while since she'd purchased any new gowns, and a pure feminine longing filled her. She knew, though, when the time came to purchase new clothing, they would be work attire such as a frock coat and, the latest rage for men, a woolen felt bowler with a contrasting hatband ribbon around the base of the crown.

Her life, and that of her aunt and brother, had been a constant battle for survival during the past year, so, when she won, she saved half of her winnings and sent half of it home to them. Her luck at the gambling tables had held out in the last two cities she'd left behind. There was still a lot more territory to cover and money to win on the way to reaching her final destination—San Francisco. Then she would send to Atlanta for her fourteen-year-old brother, Robbie, and their unmarried Aunt Lucinda.

Yet, as she perused Bozeman, a feeling of having come home assailed her. She shook her head. *No.* Bozeman was not San Francisco.

In a city like San Francisco, she knew she could make a

better life for herself and her family. Atlanta held nothing for them anymore but poverty and pestilence since the carriage accident a year ago that had taken her parents. They'd left behind a mountain of debt as well as their two children—Grace and her young brother. Grace had been forced to sell the family home. At the age of nineteen, she'd had much responsibility thrust upon her.

She kept her head turned away from her escort, not wanting to encourage further conversation. The less he knew about her the better. Hopefully, the man would believe her shy and reserved and would leave her to her thoughts. Until the buggy stopped, he thankfully did just that.

"I'm sorry. It appears our journey has ended rather precipitously. We have arrived at St. Angel's."

Precipitously? Of course. Only an educated person would use such a word in normal conversation.

Grace stared at a narrow, three-story red brick building. She read the engraved sign above the doorway. St. Angel's Home for Women.

Mr. O'Connell eased from the buggy, then assisted her to the ground. She shook out her skirts, aware of his tall, substantial body before her. Looking up, she met the gentle look on his face. Then he bowed and, with a hand at her waist, guided her up the stairs to her new home.

A tall woman dressed head to toe in gray wool opened

the door, allowing them entrance. "*Miss* Morgan, I assume," the severe woman said, closing the door behind them.

Her frosty tone would have put off any other woman. Not Grace. Looking her square in the eye, Grace murmured, "I am. And you must be Mrs. Couture."

Mrs. Couture nodded and folded her arms across her narrow chest.

Giving the sourpuss of a woman a sweet smile, Grace said, "Would you be so kind as to find someone to carry in my valises, madam?"

Mrs. Couture glared down her pointy nose at Grace. "The coach driver will do it momentarily." She swept a long look at Grace, staring at her midsection.

It took all of Grace's fortitude to remain silent under the woman's rude scrutiny.

"So," Mrs. Couture said, nodding curtly at John, "he the father, is he? How come he's not marrying you?"

two

John's narrowed eyes took in the proprietress, then Grace, his gaze settling on her stomach, which appeared slim as a young girl's. But he groaned inside as he deciphered the meaning of the woman's words.

St. Angel's Home for Women must be a place for fallen women to stay—ones who'd had the misfortune to get in the family way.

Grace raised her chin. "This gentleman is not the responsible party. Now then, I'd like to view my rooms, especially since I paid for them several months ago."

The woman sniffed. "As you wish." She turned on her heel and added, "Follow me."

Grace took a step after her. John stopped her by grabbing her elbow. "You could have told me you were..."

"Pregnant?" she said with stunning bluntness, pulling

her arm from his grasp. "Once again, sir, it's none of your business."

John scowled into her flashing eyes, then raked his fingers through his hair. "You're right. It's not. I just want to help you."

"Why? Because your mama would want you to?" She stepped away from him and headed down the hallway.

The woman was too perceptive. He couldn't help his behavior due to his upbringing, unable to leave any woman in distress. "Grace! Wait." The intimate familiarity of her name escaped him before he could prevent it.

She stopped, turned to face him. "Thank you for the offer, Mr. O'Connell. It isn't often people would think to help a stranger, especially one without apparent morals."

"If you need anything…"

"I don't require your assistance."

"I understand," he said, once again, his gaze settled on her waistline.

"Well, then, good day," she said briskly.

Once inside the buggy, he settled back with a sigh. The woman was an enigma, and he had yet to decipher her. One thing for certain, though; she needed a husband and a father for her child. Life for a single woman with a baby could be very difficult.

At twenty-three, he was old enough to marry, yet had far to go in the world to make a living before being able to provide for a wife and family. Besides, he hadn't been hit by Cupid's arrow yet, though with Grace, he had to admit, that 'arrow' had come close.

He was as chivalrous as the next man when it came to women but making a sacrifice like marrying a fallen woman surely qualified more for stupidity than chivalry, and he dismissed Grace from his mind.

Grace heaved a deep sigh of relief after John O'Connell left. As she unpacked, guilt centered deep inside her. She'd been barely civil to the man who had only been trying to help her. Then she decided she was justified in her behavior. He was performing the duties of a gentleman only because of his upbringing. She knew how he truly felt; she was a fallen woman, and he'd judged her accordingly.

She shrugged. It didn't matter. She would likely never see the handsome, dark-haired man again, anyway. What did she care what he thought of her? And even if he did care for her, she would not, could not, reciprocate his feelings. Her goal—to settle in a fine home in San Francisco with her aunt and brother—was all that mattered. Only then, afterwards, could she think about her own future, pursuing her writing, and hopefully leave gambling behind.

Tomorrow she'd pay visits to the gambling halls, asking about town as to which would offer her the best luck. The best pots. While she was skilled, a good dose of luck never hurt.

John settled into his spacious, furnished apartment located within the University of Montana campus proper. He had been hired as a full-fledged professor after earning his degree in agriculture from the University of Minnesota.

The Montana legislature had taken advantage of the federal Morrill Land Grant Act of 1862 and established the Agricultural, Mining and Mechanical Arts College. The purpose of the college was 'to promote the liberal and practical education of the industrial classes in several pursuits and professions in life.' Scientific and classical studies were not to be excluded but were of secondary importance.

John felt he'd found his place—educating young people about a way of life that was second nature to him. Not only had he received his education in the field, but he also had lived the life of a farmer. And happy he was to leave that hard life behind.

Turning to his valise, that stood in the center of the

furnished parlor, he unpacked his belongings. Besides the parlor was a small kitchen with a hotplate and an icebox.

The bedroom held a comfortable bed and a water closet with a claw-foot bathtub, a true luxury. He'd grown up on the family farm, and his father still hadn't built a water closet in the house. The outhouse they had functioned just fine, Father proudly replied to his family's complaints. Bathing in a tub will be a real luxury.

Tonight, he planned on taking his first bath. No more bathing in a big copper tub in the kitchen, as he did at home. Although his home life with his family had been happy, without any of the finer things, he'd vowed to possess those things in the near future and rise above his past poverty. Once he purchased his own home, horse and carriage and a houseful of furniture, he would send money home to better his parents' meager existence.

Pulling a notebook from the satchel holding his writing supplies, he took up a pencil and made note of a few furnishings he required. A bookcase or two to house his supply of books would be needed. His parents would be shipping his library, miniscule as it was, soon, along with other personal items he knew he wouldn't require immediately.

Sinking down into an over-stuffed armchair covered in a gold brocade fabric and trimmed with tassels, his thoughts wandered to the woman he'd met on the coach.

Grace. Lovely name—lovely woman—but ultimately disappointing, due to her condition.

He shrugged. He knew she was just one of many women he would meet while living and working in Montana. He pulled his watch fob from his waistcoat pocket and noted the time. Five-thirty was the supper hour noted in the teacher manual, and he was starving, not having eaten since morning. After tugging on his gray wool coat, he left his apartment and locked the door behind him.

When he arrived at the commons-dining area, he pulled on the door handle and found it locked. He peered inside a window, saw only darkness. As he turned away, an elderly man stalked toward him.

The man nodded and gave a gruff, "Good evening." Then he reached down and tried turning the knob. He scowled, glimpsed the time on his watch fob. "Its supper time, isn't it?"

John nodded again.

"Then why aren't the doors open?" he asked, rather accusingly.

"I've no idea," John said.

Abruptly, the man hit the side of his head and said, "It's Friday, isn't it?"

John nodded, none the wiser.

"That's why the dining room is closed."

"The teacher handbook says—"

"That it opens at five-thirty on every day *except* Friday. Friday is Cook's day off. Obviously, you didn't read the fine print."

John groaned. "Apparently not. So, where is the nearest eating establishment?"

"No idea. I rarely leave the school grounds."

The man looked John up and down, then said, "You must be new then." He stuck out his hand. "I'm Professor Roger Carlson."

"Good evening, Professor Carlson," John said cordially. "Nice meeting you," he said, and shook the proffered hand. "I'm John O'Connell."

"Can I ask how you manage meals on Friday?"

"I have some fruit and sausage in my apartment to tide me over until breakfast." With that, Professor Carlson saluted and trudged away.

A man of few words, obviously.

Unfortunately, John had no snacks in his apartment. He decided to walk to a restaurant to find his supper. He took his time, ambling up the road from the school that led to the town of Bozeman, and Main Street, having recalled seeing several small eating establishments on the ride to the college.

It was a bit of a walk, but in less than fifteen minutes, he arrived in the center of town. Bozeman appeared to be spread out with neatly boarded walkways. The town, however, was surrounded by wide open, dusty terrain. He'd have to see about purchasing a horse to thoroughly explore his new home.

The walkways grew more crowded the further west he headed. He discovered several restaurants, all on the same street, squeezed in between saloons, dry goods stores, and other businesses. The ladies carried parasols to protect their complexions as a lady would, despite the cool weather. Some men were attired in fine coats, while others wore simple chambray shirts, vests and brown cotton duck overalls—clothing appropriate for manual labor.

He paused in front of Mrs. Connor's Eatery and looked into the glass-paned window to see several customers partaking of their dinner. After he entered, an older woman wearing a white cap approached him with a smile.

"By yerself, are ye?"

Irish, he decided from her accent. He found her friendly demeanor comforting. "Yes, madam."

She waggled her finger at him. "Fine, handsome man such as yerself shouldn't be eatin' alone. Come along."

The woman showed him to a table for two next to a window overlooking the street. "The special today is Chicken Giblets with Egg and biscuits. The rest of the menu's on the board over there."

John looked over his shoulder to where she pointed

and saw several items chalked on a blackboard. In the end, he decided on the soup, roast beef, potatoes and carrots dinner.

A tiny, younger replica of the woman who had seated him arrived at his table to take his order. She smiled brightly and, instead of asking for his order, asked his name, where he was from, where he was staying. He soon realized the girl was flirting with him. He grinned and enjoyed her attentions until she got around to taking his order. Her hair was very blonde beneath her cap, her frame on the pleasantly plump side. Pretty, he'd call her, yet, as thoughts of his coach companion filled his mind, he found she didn't attract him.

Soon she returned with his chowder and a plate full of biscuits. He gulped one biscuit down, then another. He'd just raised a spoon full of chowder to his lips when he glanced out the window and saw a dapperly attired young man on the opposite side of the street.

John set down his spoon and continued to watch him. The man appeared to be a tourist exploring the establishments. Though he was a stranger, there was something familiar about him. Wearing a brown plaid suit coat with matching pants, brown boots on his feet and a brown felt derby hat on his head, the man was small. His hair must be very short since there wasn't a single strand to be seen from beneath his hat.

The man crossed the street and headed toward him, pausing outside the window to read the menu on the blackboard. Then he glanced at John, quickly turned and walked away.

Those eyes... John stilled. *The man possessed Grace's eyes!*

John came to his feet. The act of shoving his chair back, rising and leaning on the small table sent his coffee cup crashing to the floor. He jumped out of the way of its splash. Within moments, the pretty server flew to his side to clean up the mess. John thanked her, then threw several bills on the table.

Hurrying outside, he looked up the street where the man had headed and sprinted in that direction. After a dozen blocks, he wondered what he was doing. Sure, the man held more than a passing likeness to Grace, but since she'd been on his mind, it could have been his imagination. Damn that the woman seemed to always be on his mind—she'd invaded him, body and soul.

He reached a street that housed several gambling halls and saloons. John ambled past them, peering over each set of swinging doors, noting the similar structures. Lively music and raucous shouts and laughter poured from the establishments. Having been brought up by strict, God-fearing parents, he was surprised he felt an 'itch' to enter. His family had played some card games. Just for fun, of course, never for money. What was the harm in a few innocent games? Perhaps he'd stop by one of the places soon and try his hand at a game or two.

Daylight was fading. Time to head for home. Grace flittered through his mind once more. He'd courted a few women over the years. None seriously. Was he at the point in his life where he desired one particular woman in his life? Thinking of Grace and her situation, he felt sorry for her. Nodding in satisfaction, he decided pity was all he felt for her—nothing more. A tiny voice inside said, keep lying to yourself...

Gambling of any kind had been outlawed across the state of Montana. Regardless, the new legislation hadn't stopped the construction of thirty saloons in Bozeman proper alone. Most lawmen were gamblers, too, and turned a blind eye to what they considered 'harmless fun' compared to other lawlessness.

Grace sat at a table, surrounded by men at the Golden Nugget saloon. She pulled the brim of her brimmed bowler lower and surreptitiously shoved a loose strand of hair beneath it. Guessing at the price she'd pay if anyone realized she was Grace Morgan and not Gray Morrison, she was careful of her appearance. She brushed lint off her houndstooth woolen suit coat, as she awaited the next play.

Even before entering the hall, excitement had filled her at the thought of sitting down at the table and holding the cards again, hopefully the right cards.

What was it about gambling that always made her feel that way? Was it merely the enjoyment of playing the games themselves, or was it the fact she felt powerful when she won? Pragmatic always, she knew the answer was a combination of several reasons. Mostly, she enjoyed the feeling of besting a man at a man's game. After years of physical abuse at the hand of her drunken father, she'd wanted to beat men, in some fashion, at their own games. The only thing more satisfying would be revealing her womanhood to them. She shuddered at the thought of their reaction, though!

As she stared down at her cards, her heart beat at a runaway pace. Luck had found her this first night. Never had she played so well or won so much money. Mentally counting up her earnings, she decided she'd made enough now to send for her family.

Smirking at the men circling the table, she laid down her last winning hand, rising from her chair simultaneously. "It appears I've been lucky again, gentlemen," she growled in a soft, deep tone. She reached forward and swept her winnings toward her.

A hand clamped over her cowhide gloved one. The gloves were a necessity, for she knew one look at her hands and the men would realize she was a woman. She met the furious eyes of Gus Parker, a black-bearded man.

"Wait a damned minute, mister."

Grace's gaze met his, keeping her composure.

"You cheated. Everyone at this table saw you." With a dark, menacing look, he added, "Ain't that right, boys?"

Non-verbal consensus came in the form of grunts from a few. Others remained silent. One rose and left. Grace felt all eyes on her and her cheeks turned hot in a combination of anger and humiliation. Though she didn't want to feel it, fear rose in her. No one had ever accused her of cheating, and now she wasn't quite sure how to handle the situation.

Fortunately, she recalled seeing this same thing happen to a man in a saloon in Nevada. She adopted his casual manner. Shrugging her shoulders, she yanked her hand out from beneath Parker's. "Me? Cheat? Look to yourself, man, for you're an awful poker player."

Heart hammering in her chest, she dared to meet the man's eyes. Fury filled his face and spoke volumes. Not for the first time did she wish she'd learned to shoot a gun. She didn't even own one. She'd noticed how the men in town openly wore their guns. As a matter of fact, the laws clearly stated a man had a right to bear arms as long as the weapons were in clear view.

An elegantly dressed, bald-headed brute of a man appeared at her elbow. Grace saw he was one of the Nugget's owners. "What's the problem?"

"He cheated me out of five thousand, Royce. Others here can back me up."

Royce glanced at each man's face. "That true, boys? The little gentleman here cheat?"

Grace cringed at the man's description of her. The piano player had stopped playing, drinks were no longer being poured. Utter silence fell with a thud on the hall. Grace felt all eyes on her.

After a long, tense moment, Royce said, "Looks like you might be in the minority, Parker. Give the man his money and get the hell out of here."

"Damn it, Royce!" Parker bellowed.

He went silent when the saloon owner pinned him with a hard look.

The other men rose from the table and stepped away. Royce folded his arms and nodded at her. "Pick up your winnings and get out, mister. Time to call it a night."

Nodding in agreement, Grace pocketed her earnings, then turned on her heel and headed for the door. Just when she reached the swinging doors, a hard hand grabbed her elbow and whirled her around. She gasped.

Royce gave her the once-over. Finally, he leaned over and whispered, "*Mister* Morrison? I'm advising you now, *lady*, stay away from The Golden Nugget—if you know what's good for you."

Grace's eyes widened when he said softly, "Next time, be sure the glue's not visible around the whiskers."

She gave him a brisk nod before exiting the gambling hall. Her entire body shook. Dear God, she'd been caught. Yet she decided the man named Royce wouldn't reveal her identity so long as she didn't return.

Maybe the time had come to quit gambling. With the money she'd won, she could pay off her debts and still afford several months' room and board at her present domain. Best of all, she could send for her family. At long last, perhaps she could settle down and work at getting the novels she'd written published. And not write another dime-store story.

If I win a few more times, though, I'll have a better cushion. Is it worth the risk?

In less than an hour, it would be dark. She strode briskly down the street and headed for home. Stepping down from the boardwalk, she paused as a horse and rider sped by. She was midway across the street when she heard pounding hooves and squeaky wagon wheels coming toward her. Looking to her right, she saw a wagon barreling down on her and she picked up her pace.

Suddenly, a hard body slammed her to the ground. A pair of muscular arms settled around her waist and rolled her across the street just as the wagon passed by. Stunned, her face smashed into the hard-packed dirt road, Grace lifted the only part of her body she felt capable of moving —her face. The heavy body still lay atop her.

She squirmed beneath the weight and gasped aloud, "Let me up!"

The weight eased, and then a pair of hands pulled her to standing. In the dim light of dusk, Grace had no problem recognizing the big man in front of her. John O'Connell. A look of apology filled his face. "Sorry, mister. Thought you were about to become dust under those wagon wheels."

Grace scowled at him but said not a word. If she spoke, he would recognize her in an instant.

His eyes narrowed at her continued silence and averted gaze. "Grace?"

three

Grace scrutinized her surroundings, satisfied to see they were alone. The noise inside would prevent anyone from learning that the lucky Gray Morrison was actually Grace Morgan. Maintaining her identity was important if she ever needed to gamble again.

"Yes, it's me," she muttered while heat seeped into her face. Lord, what must this man think of her?

"Why are you dressed like—"

Hearing voices nearby, Grace reached up, covered his mouth with her hand, and shook her head. He nodded in understanding just as two men she recognized from the gambling hall earlier came into view.

The men looked astonished and stunned at one man's hand over the mouth of another's. They scowled at her as they passed by.

Looking at John, she said softly, "You, sir, are too observant."

He shrugged. "I'm a teacher. It's what I do best. I read, watch, listen, learn, then instruct. Besides," he added with a smile, "you have the most memorable eyes. Now, would you care to explain to me why you're dressed in menswear?"

"It's none of your business."

Drawing nearer, he said, "That won't work anymore, Miss Morgan. I've caught you red-handed."

Giving a quick look around, Grace straightened her jacket. "It appears you have the advantage at the moment, doesn't it?"

"Appears so, madam."

"I've my reasons, and that's all I'll say about it." And then, with indignation, added, "What do you think you're doing?" He was practically dragging her down the street. She yanked herself free of his grasp.

"Escorting you home." A confused look crossed his face, and he halted in front of her. "You *aren't* pregnant, are you?"

"No," she admitted.

"Then why did you lead me to believe you were? And why would you want to live in a house for women of unfortunate circumstances, anyway? What about your reputation?"

"It was cheap housing and all I could afford. As for my reputation, no one in Bozeman knows me."

Frowning, he said, "How did you manage to get by your landlady dressed like a man?"

"That," she said, "was fairly easy. As I was leaving, I explained to Mrs. Couture that I was a doctor there to pay a visit to one of the women. My landlady, thank the Lord, is not a bit observant. She didn't recognize me, unlike you."

"Yes, well, now we've got to figure out a way to get you back inside the house."

Grace raised her chin. "I'll find my own way, thank you very much."

"You will need help."

He pulled a tin box from his inside jacket pocket, opened the lid, and pulled out a cigar. They set off once more as he tucked the box away. With the cigar clamped between his teeth, he dug a match from another pocket, struck it against a brick building in passing, and lit the cigar. Grace enjoyed the silence between them, the aroma from his cigar somehow soothing her. Soon they reached her dwelling. Standing outside an iron gate, she stared up at the building.

"What is it?" John asked.

"You're right. Mrs. Couture will be suspicious at seeing me a second time."

"You'll have to change clothes then."

"I've no clothes with me other than what I'm wearing. Everything I own is in my room upstairs." Scowling, she added, "It seems I didn't plan this very well."

"I gather this is the first time you have portrayed a man, then?" He snubbed his cigar out against the gate, tucked it back inside its tin box, and stuffed it into his jacket pocket.

"No, I've done it several times. It's just that I've always taken rooms at larger hotels where no one would take much notice of another body coming and going."

John shook his head and a crooked smile crossed his lips. "Well then, I suppose there's nothing to do except take you home with me."

"I beg your pardon!"

Raising an eyebrow at her, he watched her with that mild smile.

She couldn't help considering his proposition as a solution to her dilemma. Tomorrow, when the shops opened, she could purchase a new gown, underpinnings and shoes since she had no idea how to get back into St. Angel's Home. What a complete waste of money that would be. She suddenly remembered then how she'd left the window to her room on the second floor open.

"Come around the back with me a minute." She strode briskly across the lawn and to the back of the house.

She heard John on her heels, muttering, "What in the world do you have up your sleeve now?"

Casting a quick grin at him, she whispered, "Aptly put, Mr. O'Connell. I think I've a solution as to how to get inside the house without being caught."

He groaned as he looked up at the tree to which she was pointing.

"No. Absolutely not. You're not going to climb it."

"True. I'm an abysmal climber. I'm not, but you are."

"Excuse me?" he said, sending her a narrowed look.

"What would your mama think if you didn't come to my aid in this moment of my need?"

John's jaw jutted out. "You're serious."

She nodded.

Heaving a sigh, he tore off his jacket and rolled back his sleeves.

Grace was satisfied when John, a large, masculine, magnificent specimen if there ever was one, easily climbed the tree. Just the thought of having to deal with Mrs. Couture made her shudder. Anger filled her then. She didn't owe the woman any explanations.

"Which window is it?" he called out as quietly as he could.

"You're right in front of it. Oh, John! You are the most chivalrous of men to help me this way."

"Oh-oh," he remarked.

She shouted, "What is it?"

"Quiet!" he ordered. "Mrs. Couture is in your room."

"What? Darn it!" Grace replied.

"Even worse."

"Heavens, what?"

"She's looking straight at me."

"Oh, no!"

Mrs. Couture's scream rent the air at the same time John scrambled down from the tree. On the last branch, his shoe got caught in the foliage, causing him to fall the rest of the way, landing on his ass on the hard-packed ground.

He scrambled to his feet, grabbed her arm and started running like the hounds of Hell were on their heels. When they'd put a few blocks behind them, their run slowed to a casual stroll and they walked side by side, hands buried deep in their pockets.

John glanced down at Grace and saw the smile she was trying to control. Grinning, he shook his head and roared with laughter, pausing to clutch his stomach in an effort to control himself. Grace laughed with him, snatched up his arm and pulled him into continuing their escape.

Grace shivered when a police trolley pulled by horses tore past them, horns honking.

John grimaced. "Damn, the fool woman's reported me to the police."

"Do you think she recognized you?"

He paused a moment, then said, "I don't think so. If she had, I'm guessing she would have thrown up the sash and frozen me with one of her looks, or given me a tongue-lashing, or, worse, shoved me out of the tree." He scowled at Grace as they turned a corner. "Are you satisfied now? Whatever gave you such a hair-brained idea, anyway?"

Grace shrugged. "I thought it worth a try. It seems now I've no choice but to go home with you and return in the morning for my possessions, that is after I purchase a gown. I've a feeling, after discovering I've been gone all night, Mrs. Couture won't want me staying at St. Angel's. Do you have a house?"

"I've an apartment on the University of Montana campus."

Grace's eyes widened. "You're a professor, not a teacher?"

"Same thing," he replied modestly.

"I see." She'd been right from the beginning; he was an educated man. Suddenly, she felt intimidated by the fact. Obtaining a degree in literature and writing had always been her dream—one she guessed she would never fulfill. Her parents had had little education. Her father had been a textile merchant who subsidized his meager living by gambling. Instead of bringing home his earnings, however, he spent it on drink.

Straightening her spine, she said, "I thank you for your offer and I accept, Mr. O'Connell."

"John, please."

"John," she said agreeably. She noticed how his face softened when he looked down at her. As befitted a gentleman, he no doubt wanted to take her arm. With her dressed as a man, it simply wouldn't look proper.

"Have you a spare bedroom in your apartment?" she asked.

"Unfortunately, no, but we'll figure something out."

Grace caught the heightened color of his cheeks and laughed.

His head whipped toward her, and he scowled. "What?"

"You're embarrassed at the thought of me staying with you, aren't you? You needn't have invited me, you know. I've always been a resourceful woman."

"You call dressing yourself like a man, and living in a home for wayward women *resourceful*?"

"As a matter of fact, I do."

"I call it pure stupidity," he snapped.

Anger and hurt flared through Grace at the man's audacity. How often had her own father called her stupid? How often had he called her ridiculous? Never could she please the man. She'd even taken up learning his card games and playing against him to try and earn his admiration—and love. It hadn't helped. It was only after he died a year ago that she began to think she wasn't stupid or ridiculous. He'd simply been a hateful, cruel man who happened to also be a drunkard. Her mother had tried to make up for her father's shortcomings with his children. Her attempts hadn't eased Grace's feelings of inadequacy. With her growth in confidence in the past year, she'd vowed to never allow anyone to bring her down again.

"You can take your offer..." she began, but couldn't finish. Turning on her heel, she stalked away. If she stayed, she knew she'd do something she'd regret. Bash him over the head, for one.

"Wait! Grace, stop!"

She heard his footsteps behind her and broke into an all out run, her footsteps pounding in her ears against the wooden planking of the boardwalk.

After turning two more corners, she didn't hear him any more and slowed her pace as she tried to decide where to stay for the night. She turned around to scan the street, satisfied when she didn't see him. She faced forward again, and John suddenly appeared right in front of her.

Grace screamed. "My God, you scared the ever-living... You shouldn't sneak up on people!"

"And you shouldn't have run off the way you did," he muttered. "Come home with me. Whatever I said or did, I apologize. In good conscience, I cannot allow you to roam the streets like this. It'll be dark soon. It's not safe."

Grace felt like an utter fool running off the way she had. She felt even worse when she saw the sincerity in his face. She had nowhere else to go and so, with a nod, she fell into step beside him.

Wordlessly, they arrived at the school a short time later. Grace's gaze swept the lawn before her, eying the massive brick buildings that appeared dignified and austere—places where people came to learn everything they would need to pursue their life's ambition. Excitement filled Grace at the thought of attending classes.

"What do you teach, John?"

"Agriculture."

She stared at him, eyes widening. "Truly? You mean farming?"

He nodded.

"You have farming in your blood, then?"

They walked past the last building and crossed an expanse of grass. "Yes, my family has been farming in Minnesota for three generations. Since I'm an only son, it was difficult for my father when I decided not to follow in his footsteps by actually farming the land. Luckily, two of my sisters' husbands gladly worked for my father ever since they married into the family."

"Why did you become a teacher?"

"In my seventh year in school, I had the opportunity to attend a special school of higher learning in St. Paul. I had tested well, and my teacher at the time managed to secure a full scholarship for me. My father had informed me he hadn't the money for me to attend college, but he couldn't say no to a full-paid college education. He wasn't happy about it, but my mother insisted I be given the opportunity." He smiled and added, "My father, while a hard taskmaster, would never think to make my mother unhappy, so he reluctantly consented. Moving to the city afforded me an opportunity to see more of the world. I knew after the first year I wasn't meant to be a farmer. I could teach about it. I obtained scholarships each year, so I stayed on and graduated. I had received several offers to attend colleges across the country. I chose, for my parents' sake, to stay closer to home."

"And now you're far, far away from Minnesota."

He nodded. "And enjoying every minute. It is time I led my own life." He glanced down at her. "How about you? Where are you from? I hear the Deep South in your voice."

"Georgia."

"Ah," he said. "A place I've dreamed of visiting, but haven't yet had the opportunity."

He paused outside a three-story red brick building, one of several in a row on a block, and pulled a key from his pocket. After unlocking the door, he motioned her inside.

He covertly looked around before entering behind her and closing the door.

Professor Roger Carlson stepped out from behind a tree and smirked, watching John O'Connell enter his apartment—with another man. No guests were allowed in the employees' apartments and Roger felt it his duty to report the new professor to the college's President, Randall LaFoy.

Roger wore the absent-minded professor façade well, a disguise for his true purpose at the college; per the school's administration, he'd been hired to spy on the new staff for human frailties, and that encompassed many...intriguing tasks. After years of keeping his own secrets, Roger found himself jealous of the two men—no matter what their relationship.

His eyes narrowed when he thought of the smaller man. There was something about him that bothered him, exactly *what* he had no idea. He'd find out sooner or later.

four

John snapped the door closed and leaned against it. Like a hawk watching its prey, he scrutinized his houseguest ambling through his apartment and into the parlor. An uneasy feeling had come over him as he stood outside before they entered.

He had glanced around him but hadn't noticed anything unusual. Imagination playing tricks on him, he mused, knowing well it was against house rules to have any visitors. There were common areas provided at the school for guests. But he couldn't ignore the fact that Grace had nowhere else to go.

He stayed against the door, his arms folded across his chest as he watched her examine his personal possessions. She peered down to look at a photograph of his family on a side table. Her jacket had ridden up in the back, revealing a pants-clad curvaceous bottom. Abruptly, she straightened and turned to him and he met her eyes.

"This," she said, waving her arm around the room, "is much nicer than my rooms. Standard fare for professors?"

"No. I'm subletting the place from another professor who is in Europe teaching for the school year. I was lucky."

She raised her brow. "And if you hadn't been lucky?"

Laughing, he said, "I'd be staying in one of the tiny one-room apartments in a student dormitory."

Smiling, she sank onto the end of the divan. "With the students? Now that would be interesting, you have to admit."

"True. And I very well may end up there next year, since the owner of this apartment will be returning."

"Tell me more about yourself, John O'Connell."

With a shake of his head, he sat on the opposite end of a divan. "I believe it's time you talked about yourself. What are you doing here in Bozeman? Apparently, you're alone?"

She sighed and murmured, "I gamble for a living."

"So..." he said slowly, "you were leaving that saloon where you had been gambling?" At her nod, he asked, "I hope you won then?"

"Absolutely."

"Isn't this activity risky? After all, it's against the law for a woman to gamble."

"It is, but I have no other employable skills, and I am good at gambling."

"I'd hardly call gambling a means for making a living."

"On the contrary, if one is good enough, it's very lucrative," she replied.

"Since you say you're good at it, how often do you win?" he inquired.

"About ninety-two percent of the time."

John whistled in appreciation.

"My parents didn't believe in women being educated beyond the basics of reading and writing and a bit of 'rithmetic, and how to manage a home." She sighed and added, "They expected me to marry a local boy. I refused. Attending college has always been my unfulfilled dream."

"May I ask how you learned this trade?"

"My father." He opened his mouth, but she raised her hand and stopped him. "I know, what kind of father does that to his child? He was not a very nice man—he's been gone awhile now—but he did teach me that because he found I had a natural knack for it. And I'd always had a way with numbers—counting, you know?"

"Perhaps he had an ulterior motive?"

She burst out laughing. "Right on, John! He was a horrible gambler—lost all the time. I believe he held high expectations for me. Unfortunately, he didn't live long enough to ever see me play."

"Why not attend school?" he said encouragingly.

"Lack of funds, for one thing."

"And if you had the money to pursue an education, what would your area of study be?"

"Writing—perhaps history, or literature."

John caught the vivid sparkle in her eyes. He thought of several books he would recommend her to read in the future. In the short time since they met yesterday, he'd made up his mind to pursue Grace. Everything in his life was new. New job, new home. Hopefully, a new woman.

He saw no reason why he couldn't have her in his life, and Grace fit the bill exquisitely. If he went slowly, maybe he wouldn't frighten her off. "I'm an awful host not to have offered you something to drink. Would you like coffee or a cup of tea?"

"Tea, please."

John rose to his feet and smiled down at her. "Have you eaten supper?"

"Yes. I ate at the boarding house earlier." She tilted her head to one side and gave him an assessing look that made him blush. "Can you cook?"

"Yes."

"Truly?"

"Believe it. My mother insisted I learn right alongside my three sisters."

"Unheard of!" she cried.

He laughed as he headed toward his small kitchen, saying, "Mother always said I'd make a woman a wonderful husband if I did."

John turned back to see her smile.

As he brewed a pot of tea, he was glad it was Friday. His first day of teaching wasn't until Monday. He had a few days to tour the city before beginning his work. He looked forward to his first day of teaching, but tonight he looked forward to enjoying the company of a beautiful woman. Perhaps, since Grace was also new in town, she'd allow him to escort her about during the next few days.

He carried the teapot and two small cups into the parlor. For a moment, he thought she'd left him. But he found her sitting before a chess game by the window.

After setting down the teapot, he poured them each a cup and ambled to her side. She never took her gaze from the chessboard. Carefully, he nudged her hand with the saucer and she took it from him. He sat down opposite her, watched her study the board and the position of the chess pieces. He'd been playing against himself earlier—something he did when there was no one else to share his appreciation of the game.

"Tell me you play."

She glanced up at him, then leaned back in her chair and gave a nonchalant shrug. "A little."

"Enough to offer me some competition?"

A pensive expression crossed her face. "Probably not, but I'm willing to try—if you don't..."

Watching her closely, he waited for her to finish her comment. When she didn't, he asked, "If I don't what?"

"Make fun of me and the moves I make."

John frowned. "Now, why in the world would I do that?"

She shrugged again. "It's happened before, that's all, and then I lose all my confidence."

Reaching out, John took her free hand. She gave him a startled look and started to pull her hand back. He kept it in his grasp until she stopped tugging. Smoothing the palm, he stared down at the soft, fair skin. "I'd never make fun of you. Truly. Perhaps someday you will tell me who did."

"Perhaps," she replied.

He caught the sheen of tears in her eyes and stifled his groan. Someone had hurt her—and had done a damned good job of it. He was beginning to realize so much of Grace's persona was false—purely bravado when she was a beaten down little soul.

With a curt nod, she bit her lip.

"Since you're sitting on the white side, it's your move first."

Grace was an unseasoned player, but she played with a passion he admired. Midway through their game, she stretched her arms high above her head and arched her back.

John's breath caught at the sight. Her breasts jutted out against the fabric of her man's suit jacket. Then she collapsed against the back of her chair and closed her eyes.

"You're exhausted." At her nod, he added wryly, "Thinking can be tiring." He folded his hands between his knees and leaned over the chessboard.

Her laughter exploded in the silence of the parlor. "Oh, for certain it can be."

"Have you plans for tomorrow?" he inquired as he sank against the back of his chair.

"Aside from touring the town a bit, not particularly."

"Allow me to show you about."

Grace's eyebrows shot up. "Oh! Then you know Bozeman?"

"No. But I'd enjoy learning about it and seeing it through your eyes, too, with your delightful compan-ionship."

Once again, he saw her biting her lower lip as she pondered his suggestion. Finally, she raised her gaze to his and said softly, "I think I'd enjoy that. Thank you."

John grinned. "Excellent. We'll have breakfast together, then stop by a ladies shop so that you may purchase a set of clothing. We don't want Mrs. Couture growing suspicious, do we?"

A mischievous look crossed her face. "Oh, then you don't believe my not coming home for the night would provoke any suspicions in her mind, do you?"

He kept his face as bland as he possibly could. "Not a chance."

She burst out laughing again and he joined her.

"No, you will escort me back to St. Angel's early in the morning. If Mrs. Couture tells me I must leave, so be it. I will then be obliged to find another domain."

"How will you get into your room, though?"

"Through the front door, which I should have done tonight, instead of making you climb that tree."

"You didn't twist my arm, you know."

She smiled. "I know, and it was very kind of you to come to my aid."

"If Mrs. Couture gives you any trouble, then we shall spend the day looking for another place for you to stay."

Grace sighed. "I'm afraid I can afford little by way of rent."

He studied her face for a minute. "What happened to you winning ninety-two percent of the time?" Immediately, he cursed himself for asking since her cheeks turned a brilliant red hue.

"I'm saving most of my money for travel money for my aunt and younger brother to join me once I arrive at my final destination where I hope to build a home."

"And that is..."

"San Francisco."

Deciding he shouldn't ask anything else at this point, he stated decisively, "We'll find some place you can afford."

He rose from his chair, took her elbow, and helped her to her feet. "Come, it's time to rest." Even in the parlor's dim lighting, he saw her face color a charming shade of pink. "You may take my bed. The divan will be fine for me."

Grace stopped and gave him a wide-eyed look. "Oh! I'll take the divan. Besides, you are much too tall for it."

"Absolutely not. You are my guest. What sort of host would I be if...?"

"No. I won't stay if you insist, John. I won't."

Lord but the girl was stubborn!

"All right, then, I'll make up the divan for you."

"Just a pillow and a light blanket should suffice."

When John returned from his bedroom with a blanket and pillow in his arms, he stopped dead in his tracks. Grace had removed her jacket and was in the process of shrugging out of her waistcoat. Her back was to him and he found himself greedily staring at her womanly backside clad in the plaid men's pants and the narrow tapering of her waistline in a crisp white shirt that was still tucked into the waistband.

Lord, how had she fooled anyone into believing she was a man? With her pretty curves, it was impossible.

John cleared his throat, and she turned to him and took the blanket and pillow. "Thank you," she said softly, proceeding to make up her bed.

"I feel terrible about this," he murmured.

She whirled to face him. "Why?"

"As I said, you are my guest."

"Not by your choice, but by chance. Thank you for the offer." She sank down on the divan and added awkwardly, "Well then, good night, John."

"Yes, good night," he said, hearing the reluctance in his own voice. Stepping back a few steps he stared down at her as she lifted her legs and curled onto her side, her head on the pillow. It was only then he noticed she'd removed her shoes. His heart lurched when he saw the holes in her white stockings—women's stockings. Her dainty feet and sweetly feminine body deserved much better attire.

John tossed and turned, in one moment pulling the covers to his chin, in the next yanking them down. Hot and cold tore through his body, all because of the beautiful woman asleep on his divan. God, what did she think he was, a bloody saint? No more, he decided, wrenching himself into a sitting position.

His conscience warred with his upbringing. He was a gentleman, but a gentleman had limits. He shed the guilty feelings as he thought of her in his bed, making love to her. Immediately, his excitement faded. She hadn't shown any romantic interest in him whatsoever, and he sank back on his bed, feeling low and irritable.

John shot up in bed though when he heard voices calling to him, and a banging on his apartment door. Damn. It was the middle of the night! Donning a long velvet robe, he tied the belt as he left the bedroom. With a quick glance, he noted Grace sitting up on the divan, rubbing her sleepy eyes.

"John? Someone is at the door."

"Yes, I know," he gritted out, "and they'd better have a damned good reason for waking us."

She didn't need to know he hadn't fallen asleep yet.

He unlocked the door and yanked it open, surprised to find the President, Randall LaFoy, and Professor Roger Carlson on his doorstep.

"Gentlemen?" John said as he moved outside, closing the door behind him.

LaFoy stood directly below John, a scowl in place. "Professor? You've yet to start your first day of work, and I've heard some unsettling news about you."

Frowning, John replied, "I don't understand."

Before John could react, Professor Carlson moved up, jostling past LaFoy and shoving John out of the way, storming into the apartment. John followed him, cursing in silence, groaning when Carlson stopped directly in front of the divan where Grace lay buried beneath her blanket—every inch of her body.

"See!" Carlson accused, pointing at her huddled form. "He's been caught red-handed! It appears our illustrious new professor is a lover of men."

John felt light-headed at the man's condemning words. *Damn!* Why hadn't he followed his own feelings earlier in the evening? But then, what could he have done differently?

Meeting the accusing look on LaFoy's face, John said, "Allow me to explain, sir."

"Go ahead," President LaFoy said.

"This is all quite innocent." John moved to stand in front of Grace, blocking her from their view.

Before he could continue, he felt a nudging against the back of his leg. Looking behind him, he groaned when he saw Grace had thrown off her blanket and was sitting up. Then she stood beside him and wound her arm around his waist.

"Allow me, darling," she said, her sweet voice filtering through the parlor.

five

"John and I wondered how long we could keep our secret." Grace shrugged and added, "Unfortunately, not long enough."

John's heart skipped a beat at the genuine look of adoration on Grace's face—or she was an actor blessed with incredible skill.

"Shall we tell them of our upcoming nuptials?"

Stunned by her words, John could only give a slow nod in response.

"A week from now we'll be marrying at...at..." *Oh, Lord, I have no idea of the name of any churches in the vicinity!*

"Old St. Mary's Cathedral next Sunday," John inserted.

"Yes, that's it," she murmured.

LaFoy glared at Carlson. "What is this? This is the third

time you've screwed up in the past year. I have half a mind to force you to leave, professor."

Carlson blustered, "But you can see why I believed he was a man!" He pointed at Grace's attire, his lined faced crumpling.

"I don't understand," John said.

"Professor Carlson believed you had invited a person— no matter the gender—to stay in your apartment, which of course is against the college's rules."

"But we're marrying, sir, and I couldn't live another moment without Grace being with me," John protested.

Grace thought how easily he'd said the words and she felt her cool heart melting even more toward John. But it wasn't possible to fall in love with someone in such a short time—was it?

LaFoy smiled at Grace. "Of course you love her. I don't blame you a bit, and I am glad to see you were being a gentleman by having her sleep on the divan. I will not inquire as to why she's attired in men's clothing." His smile slipped when he added, "Unfortunately, I cannot bend the school's rules. I'm afraid you will have to go, Mr. O'Connell."

"I'll leave, of course. I knew the consequences of my actions beforehand."

Grace protested, "But that's not fair!"

She caught the warning look John sent her when he

added, "Providing you write me a letter of recommendation."

"How can I when you've not actually put in a day of work with us?" LaFoy asked.

"You hired me, didn't you? Based on letters from professors at the University of Minnesota. No one need know I didn't actually fill the position."

Eyeing John a moment, LaFoy turned to Professor Carlson. "Leave us. I'll deal with you later."

Almost feeling sorry for the elderly professor, Grace watched him draw himself up, yank down his waistcoat and leave the apartment. Her gaze fixed now on President LaFoy, who seemed to be sizing up John.

"You know, I like a man of integrity, a man who faces up to the consequences of his mistakes, which you've done quite admirably. I'm keeping you on, Professor O'Connell. You start Monday, as usual, unless you've some objection to staying?"

"No objections, sir," John replied.

"Good." The man turned and headed for the door. After opening it, he paused on the threshold, looked over his shoulder and gazed at Grace. "I can't allow your fiancée to stay here, however, so you will need to escort her home."

Grace felt the tenseness in the room between the two men.

"She has nowhere else to go," John finally murmured.

Returning to her side, LaFoy took her elbow. "Then you shall return home with me, my dear. My Margaret will put you up until your marriage on Sunday."

"I'd like a few words with Grace alone before she leaves," John said.

"Of course you do. I'll be right outside."

Once LaFoy left, closing the door behind him, Grace latched onto John's arm. "I have no desire to go home with him! Why were you so agreeable?"

John grasped her shoulders and met the panic-stricken look in her eyes. "This is the best solution to your dilemma. You can't return to St. Angel's, and going home with LaFoy, where his wife can care for you, is the perfect solution. Besides, I won't jeopardize losing this job. This is my livelihood, and if I lose it, how will I provide for my wife?"

"What wife!" Grace blurted.

"I meant my soon to be wife—you."

"I'm not marrying you, John, or anyone else for that matter," she groaned. "This is all make-believe. I'll play along, as long as I must, to save your position, but that's all."

He frowned. "I'm afraid we'll be marrying then on Sunday, for there's no other way out of this predicament."

His frown diminished as he said softly, "It won't be all that bad, you know."

Grace gasped in surprise when he swept her close against his body until her toes barely scraped the floor. His lips slanted across hers, tantalizing hers softly in one moment, ravaging them in the next.

They parted when they heard LaFoy outside the door say, "You about done in there, young people?"

"Just about," John murmured. He lowered Grace to the floor, his eyes on her the entire time, his lips curved into a smile.

Grace touched her lips with shaky fingers, her eyes wide. She backed away from him, then turned and ran to the door. Just as her hand covered the knob, his hand came down over it. Heat tore through her when he encompassed her in his arms, pulled her against him, and nuzzled her neck with his soft lips as he turned the knob, his hand still on top of hers. He released her just before the door completely opened. LaFoy nodded at John as he took Grace's arm and escorted her away.

John returned to his bed. Lying on his back, his arms behind his head, he thought about his options; marry Grace and keep his position, don't and he'd lose it, which he couldn't afford to do. He'd worked too hard to get to this place and point in his life. She would have to marry him. Afterwards, once he'd proven himself to President

LaFoy, they could obtain an annulment, for he'd made the decision not to consummate the marriage. Yes, Grace would cooperate once she knew he meant the arrangement to be a temporary one. With that last thought, he rolled over and fell asleep again.

John didn't see Grace the next morning. He appeared on LaFoy's doorstep to discover she'd gone shopping with Margaret LaFoy.

John left LaFoy's home with his hands in his pocket, thinking how he'd better make his way to St. Mary's Cathedral. Being raised a Catholic, he knew he'd have to gain a special dispensation to waive the typical banns of marriage announced over a month's time in a parish. Guilt plagued him then. He didn't feel a bit uncomfortable marrying Grace with plans of annulling the marriage later. Born and raised a christian man of morally strong values, this idea was not an easy one for him to swallow. But he truly had no other choice.

Luckily, he found a friend and fellow Irishman in Father Thomas O'Halloran. An hour later, he left the church with the special license in hand. Grace would have no choice but to marry him now.

That evening they supped together at Johnson's

Eatery. After supper, he ordered a scotch whiskey while Grace drank her tea. He stared at her, now dressed lavishly in a silk gown of Margaret LaFoy's choosing. John admitted the woman possessed excellent taste. The skirt was fashioned of panels of russet and cream striped satin. The neckline was not too high or too low. It offered just a glimpse of Grace's creamy skin. His hands itched to reach out and stroke her sweetly curved neck, and lower, but he kept them on the table, one hand still holding the glass.

Irony filled him then. How would he keep his hands off her once they married? Once he knew in the eyes of the law and God above she would be his for the taking? He would be strong—he would have to be.

His eyes swept appreciatively over her petite frame. "I see you had a productive day."

"I most certainly did," she said, a small smile tilting up her lips.

"Hopefully you were discreet about us?"

"Of course." She frowned. "It was my idea in the first place to pretend we were engaged."

"Yes, you were very quick on your feet about that."

She shrugged. "I've had lots of practice."

He raised his brows. "What? You've been in similar situations before?"

"Not that particular one. I mean, at the gambling

tables. One must be quick on the draw, so to speak, in order to come out ahead."

"I see." Idly, John rubbed the rim of his glass. "Do you enjoy gambling?"

As though sensing a trap, John noticed her hesitation. Finally, she said, "Yes, I do. But I'm able to stop whenever I like."

"Why do it then? Why not find respectable work?"

"I've already told you I have no skills. For a woman, there aren't all that many types of work to do that afford decent pay. Besides, it's temporary."

Deciding against pressing her further, he said, "Good. I'm glad." His mind turned to an item of greater importance; convincing Grace of the necessity to marry him.

"John, I really must return to St. Angel's Home. I'm worried whether, after having been gone for over a day and a half, Mrs. Couture will even allow me back inside."

"You don't have to return there. You're marrying me, remember?"

She leveled her gaze on him. "No, I'm not."

"But you reciprocated my kisses yesterday, and didn't you just admit it had been your idea, after all?"

"That was a ruse of the moment, that's all." She sighed. "I realize now I should never have done it."

The serious expression in her eyes was colored with guilt, as well it should be. After all, he'd helped her, hadn't he? If he hadn't shoved her out of the way of the oncoming traffic, she'd be dead. The least she could do was marry him—even if it would be temporary. Somehow, that idea of temporary instead of permanent didn't sit well with him.

He took her hand in his. "I've already acquired the license. And don't forget about my position at the college."

She slid her hand from his and crossed her arms across her bosom. "Perhaps President LaFoy will understand sometimes things don't work out between people." Her expression turned eager and he could almost see the wheels turning in her head as a story developed. "Yes! That's it. You could tell him we broke off the engagement. And you may put the full blame on me."

"I didn't want to press you on this but, simply put, you owe me Grace." Grace's jaw gaped as he continued, "All I'm asking for is a temporary marriage."

She looked at him suspiciously. "I don't understand."

"I'll give you an annulment once I've proven myself to President LaFoy."

"So we wouldn't consummate the marriage?"

He shook his head, chagrinned to see her cloudy expression clear.

"And what's in it for me, pray tell?" she said.

Leaning forward, he stared into her eyes, trying to see

what lay behind them. "Haven't I already saved your skin more than once? Like I said, you owe me."

After a long moment, she said, "You are right." She appeared deflated as she continued, "But as soon as Sunday is over, I'll be leaving for San Francisco. I'll leave it to you to explain to President LaFoy my leaving. Understood?"

"Yes. But why must you leave so quickly?"

"I have an aunt and young brother waiting in Atlanta for me to send money enough so they may travel to San Francisco, which is our final destination."

John sank back in his chair. "Good reason, I must admit. Are both of your parents gone, then?"

"Yes. They died in a carriage accident a year ago."

Ah! Now this answer made sense to him. Still he asked, "Why San Francisco?"

"More opportunities."

"For gambling?"

"True, there is that." She sighed. "But I promised my aunt I would stop gambling once I'd saved enough money to send for them."

"And then how will the three of you live?"

John noted the flash of red in her cheeks and she worried her bottom lip.

"Remember 'the penny dreadful' I was reading on the coach?"

He nodded. "Go on."

"I was reading my competition."

A slow grin crossed his lips. "You were? Ah, I think I know where this is heading. You did say you wanted to attend school for writing and literature, didn't you?"

"Yes, but I've already published three."

"Three what?"

"Penny dreadfuls," she murmured.

John opened his mouth in amazement. "You are telling the truth, aren't you?"

"Don't let anyone tell you there's a fortune to be made as an author. There isn't, and I'm proof of it, otherwise I wouldn't be gambling."

"I would never have guessed. You hardly seem the type of woman to sit still several hours a day penning a novel, that's all."

"Why do you say that?"

"Because of the chances you've taken in your life. Dressing as a man, gambling, which is a man's game, taking up residency in a home for unwed mothers, asking me to climb trees. You are full of mischief, sweetheart," he said with a laugh.

She shrugged. "I admit I have always been a mischief-maker, but you are wrong about my being inattentive. I am quite able to sit for hours at a time and write the story ideas that keep spinning through my head. Why, I've written so long my hand has gone numb."

"My, Lord! Do you mean to tell me you write in long hand?"

Her brows went up. "How else would I write my stories down?"

"With a type writing machine, of course."

"Oh, how I'd love to own one, but I can't afford it. Someday, perhaps."

"Marry me, Grace. I promise you this. I cannot give you the money you require immediately. I won't be receiving my pay for a month, but I will help you once I do."

She groaned and said, "I can't wait a month! Already my family has been waiting six months for me to send for them. They have little income, but what my aunt earns working as a seamstress, and my brother's small earnings as a blacksmith's boy."

John sighed and rose from his seat. He dug some bills from inside his jacket pocket and laid them on the table. "Come, then. I'll escort you to St. Angel's Home."

six

"Get out," were the only words a frosty Mrs. Couture uttered upon allowing Grace to enter St. Angel's Home.

Within quarter of an hour, Grace found herself, and her luggage, being loaded into a wagon once more. When she'd gone gambling the previous evening, she'd left behind her outer coat. Now she dug around in the pocket —the one with the small hole in the lining—stunned to discover her money earned in past cities was missing! Mrs. Couture, or someone else in that household, had taken it, she surmised. Having to start over again filled her with dismay. How she wanted to go back and accuse the woman, but who would believe her? Thankfully, she had the money she'd won the night before. She would need to spend another night gambling in order to have enough money to send for her brother and aunt. She kept her plans to herself, guessing John would put up a fuss about it.

At least she had a home to return to at the Lafoy's. Now, standing outside President Lafoy's home, Grace was right; John scowled and lectured her as he walked toward the Lafoy's front door.

"No more gambling. Just sit still until after we're married and I receive my first pay. Then I'll give you money to send for your family. You may pay me back once you sell another book."

Scowling back at him, she said, "You can't order me about, John. I'll be leaving for San Francisco Monday morning since I've already purchased my coach and train tickets. I don't need your money, much as I appreciate the offer." She gave him a tentative smile, reached out, and grasped his hand. "Thank you, though, for thinking of me."

Reaching up on tiptoe, she gave him a quick peck on the cheek, then stepped inside, shutting the door firmly behind her, before he could say another word. She was thankful she didn't run into Margaret or LaFoy. Once she reached her room, she sank down on the bed and couldn't help the tears seeping from her eyes and sliding down her cheeks.

Would she ever find such a kind, chivalrous man like John in her life again? She should marry him! But then, she knew the reason he'd proposed; he couldn't afford to lose his new teaching position—not because he was madly in love with her. She couldn't blame him a bit. Guilt overwhelmed her when she thought about the possibility of him losing his position at the college, and she came to a decision.

She'd gamble tonight and, if her luck held out, she'd win as much money as she had the first time. Then she'd marry John—long enough for him to prove his worth to President LaFoy. Within a few weeks, she had no doubts he'd establish himself. Then she'd file for an annulment, leave for San Francisco then, after settling into a permanent place, she'd send for her aunt and brother.

John was correct; she owed him for his help. A small voice inside her said, *Liar!* She was falling in love, pure and simple. But she couldn't allow herself to get sidetracked from her goal of securing a home for her family. Then she could tend to her own happiness.

An hour later, Grace sat at a table in the Lucky Duck Saloon a few blocks down the street from The Golden Nugget, dressed in her menswear, playing a final round of poker. Her heart beat a quick staccato as excitement roared through her. She'd won again, every hand, and now, with this one hand, she knew it would be her last. She had more than enough money to send for her family and buy a house in San Francisco for the three of them.

The man to her left threw down his cards. "Shit!" he exclaimed and left the table.

One by one, she called each man's bluff, and they tossed in their cards. She collected her winnings and jauntily left the saloon. She could hardly wait to tell John she would marry him after all, providing he stuck to the agreed few weeks of marriage, followed by an annulment.

At the corner, she started across the road when suddenly her arms were taken in a hard grip. Her head snapped up to look at the man on her right—one of the men she'd won against this evening. The man on her left, though, made her go dizzy with fright. Gus Parker! The man she'd won so much money playing against the night before last.

"Where you goin' so fast, little man," he said, his lips turned up into a near toothless smile.

She recoiled, trying to pull her arm away, but he kept a firm grip on her.

"You ain't goin' anywhere, mister, but around the corner here so we can have us a little talk."

"I got nothin' to say to you," Grace said, lowering her voice to a baritone-pitch.

"He'll change his mind, won't he, Rufus?"

The man on the other side of her laughed raucously by way of reply.

Night had fallen, and now Grace started sweating and struggling harder as they reached the last building, then turned a corner and went around to the back of it. Gus stopped. "Just hold him for me, Rufus."

"Whatcha gonna do?" the other man asked as he jammed a hand against each of Grace's shoulders, slamming her against a building.

Gus sent an evil grin at Grace, which she caught beneath the moon's rays beaming down on his raw, grisly face. "Just gonna show him a bit of Montana hospitality, is all."

She nearly lost her supper when she felt Gus rub his chest against her body. *My God!* Had he guessed she was a woman, after all? Grace struggled for release, to no avail. Rufus had her shoulders pinned against the building. Gus unbuttoned her suit coat, and she kicked out, connecting with his shin.

"Damn it!" Gus cursed. "Didn't I tell you to hold him still?"

"How?" Rufus demanded. "I can't hold all of him. Just watch out for his legs. Geez, he's just a little mite of a guy, for crissakes!"

"Kick me again, you bastard, and I'll shoot you where you stand," Gus growled at Grace.

When he bent down and his hand went to her belt buckle, she kicked him again.

"Fuck!" Gus growled. "He gave me a bloody nose!" he wailed, holding his bloody appendage. "Turn him around!"

Rufus let go of Grace. She took two steps but was grabbed from behind once more. Rufus slammed her against the building and her nose struck the wood. She bit her lip, not wanting to scream, for then they'd know she was a woman and it could go even worse for her. For certain, she decided, she was in for a beating, at the least. She had second thoughts, though, when her belt was ripped from her pants and pulled down, followed quickly by her long johns.

"Bend him over that there horse trough, Rufus," Gus growled.

Grace screamed a long piercing howl that rent the night when she was pulled away from the wall and tossed across the empty trough, flailing her arms. Her feet didn't quite touch the ground, and she kicked at the air with her bare legs, screaming again at her untenable position.

"Hear that, Gus? He squeals like a girl!"

"Yeah, ain't that somethin'? Get him away from the gambling halls and he's nothing but a cowardly, whimpering woman, ain't he? Here's what we do to little boys like you who think they're too big for their britches," Gus warned.

She screamed again—louder this time when she felt a finger shoved ruthlessly between her buttocks.

"Why, he's tight as can be. What do you think about that, Rufus?"

"What you talkin' about? You ain't plannin' on sodomizing him, are you?"

"Sure do. That'll teach him."

"What if he ain't clean?" Rufus asked.

Gus grumbled, "Yer right, damn it all. Well, a beatin' will have to do."

Her arms were ruthlessly pulled behind her back and tied together, her shoulders aching from the confinement. Grace shrieked at the top of her lungs when she heard someone shouting her name, the sound coming from around the front of the building.

Astonished, Grace realized the two men hadn't heard the voice, and she screamed louder.

"Shut him up, Rufus!"

Her stomach hurt when a knee jammed into the middle of her back, and a ball of fabric was stuffed inside her mouth and held in place with another piece.

"Grace!"

John! Her mind screamed. *Help me!*

Tears of anger, frustration and fear slid down her

cheeks when the first lick from what she guessed was her belt crossed her ass. It struck again and pain tore through her body as she struggled furiously to escape.

Suddenly, a roar unlike anything she'd ever heard before rent the air. Thuds and grunts sounded, first on one side of her, then on the other. She heard more grunts and groans as she struggled to gain her feet. When she couldn't, she turned her head far enough to one side to see John standing nearby, hands curled into fists at his sides, his position a fighting one as he stood over the two men who'd assaulted her, both of them appeared unconscious in the dirt.

John was a big man with a scholarly bent, but she never doubted his strength for a moment. He'd been raised on a farm, and done hard, physical work. Rufus and Gus hadn't stood a chance. He must have realized the men were not going to rise, for he dropped his fists and, in a few strides, came to her side and helped her to her feet. Bending down, he gently eased her undergarments and pants up. She nuzzled her nose against the softness of his chambray-clad chest as he eased the buttons of her pants through the holes, dressing her carefully as he would a child.

He stepped back from her, took her shoulders in his hands. She peered up at him and saw the worry on his handsome face. "Grace! You all right, honey?"

She nodded and then closed her eyes in grateful silence as she slipped into darkness.

The two men who'd assaulted her were thrown in jail, yet it didn't give Grace the comfort and ease she expected. John reassured her with time she'd forget about the attack. She hoped so yet had a feeling she'd suffer nightmares for years to come. Never had she felt so defenseless. She must do something about that condition, she decided, knowing she couldn't always count on John or any other 'knight in shining armor' to come to her defense.

As she lay in her bed at the LaFoy's with her eyes closed, she felt the warmth of the rising sun filling the room. She stretched luxuriously, loathe to rise except one thought giving her the impetus to do so; on this bright and clear autumn Sunday, she was getting married.

John had gently questioned her about the attack. She'd managed to give him a coherent reply, though she'd felt cold inside. He'd been furious when she'd told him why she'd gambled again; that her money had been stolen at St. Angel's Home. She discouraged him from confronting Mrs. Couture about it, nor would she allow him to report the incident to the town sheriff.

The only good thing was she still had the money she'd

won last evening—enough to send for her aunt and brother.

When John left her at the LaFoy's last evening, he'd reminded her about their marrying the next day. She'd agreed, surprised to see the joy creasing John's face, followed by blazing heat of desire in his eyes. Was it possible he wanted her for another reason, aside from the need to maintain his position? For one fleeting moment, Grace imagined what it would be like to be married to him in truth. Shaking the nonsensical idea from her head, she reminded him that their marriage would be one in name only—and temporary—at that. She'd heard the reluctance in his voice, but he'd agreed.

She rose and bathed in the bathing room at the end of the hallway, dressing in a day gown until after she'd had breakfast. She would then change into the cream satin gown that her mother had worn on her wedding day twenty years ago. Grace hadn't packed it at first, since she'd had no one to marry her, but then found she couldn't leave it behind. Breakfast with the Lafoys was filled with chatter from Margaret. "Why, I can't recall when we had a marriage in town, can you, dear?" she asked her husband.

President LaFoy said distractedly, his eyes on the front page of his newspaper. "Can't recall, sweetheart."

Grace grinned and thought how sweet the two of them were together, wondering what it would be like breakfasting with John every day. The thought filled her with sadness as she would have only one more day with him for she secured tickets for Monday's leaving. She decided then she'd change them, for she knew she owed John much for saving her life and coming to her aid. She'd stay a month. Heaven help her, would she want to leave though, at the end?

seven

John arrived by noon on Sunday to escort her to the church. Through a living room window, she watched him jump down from a shiny carriage and make his way up to the door. She opened the door just as he reached it.

"Hello," he murmured.

"Good morning," she whispered and looked down to find he held a beautifully made, delicate wreath of flowers. Tears filled her eyes as she examined it, a delicate band of fresh white roses. No man had ever given her flowers before.

"It's for your head," he murmured, handing it to her. "I didn't know if you had a veil or not..."

"I don't." She raised her eyes to his and smiled, swiping away the tears. "Thank you. It's—it's beautiful."

Though Mrs. LaFoy, upon learning Grace had her mother's gown with her, but no veil, had offered to purchase her one, she'd declined. She just didn't want anyone spending money on a wedding when the marriage most likely wouldn't last.

He held out his arm with a brilliant smile. "Shall we?"

With a nod, she called into the house, "We'll see you at the church, Mr. and Mrs. LaFoy!"

She heard rumbling voices reply as she shut the door, placed her hand on John's arm, and they made their way to the carriage with a gold swirling design on the side. An enormous horse—of a type she'd never seen before—was hitched to it. Pausing beside the animal, she examined it, noticed the shaggy hair above its hooves and said, "I don't believe I've ever seen such a large, unusual looking horse."

"It's a Clydesdale. They've been here in our country since around 1845 or so. They come from Scotland originally. Used mostly for farm work, pulling—that sort of thing. I know my father had wanted one on our farm but could never afford one."

She raised her brow as she joined him at the carriage entrance. "I have heard of the breed but never saw one until now. He's a rather big brute, isn't he? But quite lovely," she added.

John chuckled. "I think he'll be able to get us to the church just fine."

She started to lift her skirts when he stayed her.

"Hold up a minute, Grace." He went around the back, reached inside, and pulled out a set of wooden stairs. "This will make it easier."

She smiled, pleased with his being so thoughtful, and placed a hand on his arm once more, then climbed the four steps, settling into a comfortably cushioned bench seat. The carriage also had a bonnet covering, and she observed John raise it up and clamp it into position.

He picked up the steps and replaced them, then easily climbed up beside her.

"You didn't buy this conveyance, did you?" she asked, hearing the worry in her own voice, hoping he hadn't spent his money on something so luxurious.

He shook his head. "Rental place down the street. I knew President LaFoy owned a small two-person convenance only so, you know, I had to find a way to get my bride to the church, after all."

She laughed along with him, then her smile weakened away as she thought about how short their marriage would be. She sighed.

As he guided the horse down the street, she caught him glancing at her often.

Grace glanced down at her gown, then looked up to find he was still staring at her.

"What? Is there something wrong with my dress?" Her

NANCY PIRRI

voice quivered—she'd heard the unsure tone of it. Did he hate the dress on her?

"You look stunning, but then I thought you looked rather dapper in your men's attire," he replied cheekily.

Catching the glint and humor in his eyes, her smile widened. "Thank heavens, because this was my mother's wedding dress and the only one I own."

He nodded and focused now on the street as he drove them to the church—no more than a ten-minute drive.

He looked especially handsome in a navy serge suit, white starched shirt and matching tie around his neck. She sighed, wondering how she could make him a permanent part of her life, half tempted to ask him to go to San Francisco with her, though San Francisco didn't seem quite as appealing as it had in the past. Why couldn't she make a home for them here in Bozeman? She could write anywhere in the world if she wanted to—why not Bozeman?

Opportunity, she reminded herself. San Francisco was the city her aunt and brother had convinced her would be the place for them. Besides, other than the fact John needed her to save his position, he hadn't declared himself to her in any way. For all she knew, he despised her and kept the fact well-hidden due to his upbringing. She guessed he wouldn't have offered marriage if they hadn't been caught together at his dwelling by Professor Carlson.

But then she thought how often his sincere, warm eyes settled on her, thought of how she'd made him laugh, and knew he was far from indifferent to her. She looked up at him then when he covered her hand with one of his.

"Nervous?" he asked.

She smiled. "A bit, I suppose, like any bride."

"You are far from being just any bride. You're *my* bride."

"Temporarily," she softly reminded him.

He looked away, but not before she caught the irritated look in his eyes. She found herself staring at his profile. How he'd said those words, his voice laced with possession—*his* bride! Shivers of delight slid down her spine, for she found she enjoyed his possessive tone. Was it possible he wanted her as much as she wanted him? She frowned then. *What is wrong with me? I am falling madly in love with a man I've known only two days.*

They soon arrived and John headed the horse and carriage directly toward a long hitching post outside the church. He set the brake, jumped down, tied up the horse and assisted Grace. She was astonished to see several other wagons, carriages, and horses as she walked toward the entrance, her reticule and crown of flowers in hand.

Frowning, she looked up at John as he took her arm. "Oh! The church appears to be bursting at the seams."

"Yes, we're arriving a bit early, before the Sunday

service ends. It will be done shortly, however, and then we'll marry."

Heads turned as they entered the church. Grace noticed several people—men, in particular—she'd met in the saloons. Breathing a sigh of relief, she remembered then she'd been dressed as a man. It was unlikely they'd recognize her. Midway down the aisle, John stopped beside a pew. President LaFoy and his wife, Margaret, slid down, allowing them a place to sit.

Grace whispered to Margaret, "How did you end up arriving before us?"

Leaning conspiratorially toward Grace, Margaret said, "We took the short cut only we know of."

Grace raised her brow in response just as John whispered in her ear. "They've agreed to witness our marriage."

"Oh!" Grace hadn't even thought about that necessity.

Soon the Mass ended, and Grace found herself standing beside John at the altar, having donned the crown of roses and a bouquet of flowers provided thoughtfully by Margaret.

The priest, Father Thomas O'Halloran, was red-faced and grinning like a fool as he stood before them. After they said their vows and John placed a narrow gold band on Grace's third finger on her left hand, John faced Grace, his eyes sparkling as he leaned down and kissed her trembling lips. Grace had to stop herself from groaning her pleasure and remained still as she accepted his kiss.

Astonishment filled Grace then when she abruptly stepped back from John at the thunderous applause in the church. Several of the parishioners decided to stay for the vows and, even though Grace knew none of them, she was happy. It felt like a real wedding. It *had* been a real wedding, she mused.

The LaFoys insisted on taking them to dinner at Johnson's Eatery again. They all had the special of the day—only ten cents a meal—veal cutlets and potatoes and corn accompanied by steamy hot dinner rolls and butter.

That evening, as Grace settled into John's apartment, she asked herself why she couldn't latch on to some happiness for the next few weeks for herself. While she'd never experienced love-making, she was no green girl. She'd craved a man's loving—had wanted it for a long while. Perhaps San Francisco could wait a bit longer.

As she watched her new husband remove his fine jacket and loosen his tie, sliding it from around his neck, her heart sped. Handsome, and chivalrous, well described John.

After draping his jacket over the end of the divan, he turned to her, settling his hands on his hips. He smiled and said softly, "Now what shall we do?"

Before the words were out of his mouth, Grace rose

from the divan and went into his arms, as if it were something she did every day. His lips crushed hers, and he groaned his need for her. She returned his kisses, winding her arms around his neck as she stood on tiptoe, gasping when he easily picked her up and started walking down the short hallway with her.

No words did they speak. John's kisses and murmurings in her ear lit a fire within Grace that threatened to explode into a fiery inferno, so great was her need for him. With a gentleness that amazed her, John removed her clothing, his eyes paying homage to each delicious part of her body he revealed.

He sat beside her on his bed and stared at her for the longest time. Her initial embarrassment diminished when she saw the reverent look in his eyes as she lay naked before him.

"Your turn now," she whispered, anxious to see his body.

Within seconds, he'd ripped off his clothes, leaving them on the floor in a heap beside the bed. He stood before her in naked glory, his face turning a shade of pink when she looked him over from head to toe. Her eyes widened then on the staff between his muscular thighs. My Lord, she hadn't realized men were so...so big! Worry settled over her and she bit her lip and looked away.

Grace felt the side of the bed dip, then looked down to

see he'd planted his hand on the bed near her waist. Her eyes helplessly traveled up from his wrist to his sinewy forearm, ending at the bulging of thick muscles in his chest and shoulders.

"I'll be gentle as I can be," he said.

She darted an anxious look at him. "How did you know that was what I was thinking?"

He kissed her lips. "Your face is an open book. Think of it this way, our making love will make excellent fodder for your next penny dreadful, don't you think?"

Her worries immediately left, and she laughed and wound her arms around his neck as he came over her. "I hadn't thought of that, but you're right!"

He kissed her once more, his lips tracing a path of moist heat from her lips to her neck, down over her bare breasts, pausing to nibble at one nipple, then down to her very core. When he slid lower, she groaned as he suckled the delicate place between her thighs. She didn't resist when he raised her knees, tucked her legs over his shoulders, and laved her core with his tongue. Within moments, she felt her world spinning out of control, her body stiffening with desire.

"Wait, John," she gasped, trying to pull her legs from where he'd propped them over his shoulders, uncertain about her feelings—and her growing arousal.

He tightened his hands around her thighs, held her in

place. "Stay put," he murmured. "A bit longer," he added softly.

At his gentle tone, she tried to relax, her eyes tightly closed as she concentrated once more on his lovemaking. Thank God one of them seemed to know what to do, and it wasn't her! Unlike her, obviously, he'd done 'this' before.

Grace had written about men and women in love but had yet to experience the act—the ultimate 'little death'—which now swarmed over her body. She shivered and tingled from head to toe, then she went rigid when everything in her consciousness settled on the area between her thighs, rippling shivers through her lower extremities. Tighter and tighter were the sensations until they burst. She gasped, her body spasming over and over again. Exhausted, her body drenched with sweat from their lovemaking, she smiled lethargically when she felt him crawling up her body, his hands lifting her thighs once more. Her eyes shot open when he slid inside her slowly. Clutching his forearms, she bit her lip at the full feeling of his entry.

When he'd slid as far in as he could, he pulled back, then jerked his hips forward. Grace gasped at the one startling sharp pain, then relaxed when he proceeded to move in and out of her channel with amazing softness, slowly, carefully.

"You are so hot, so wet for me," he said, kissing the side of her neck. "I didn't hurt you too much, did I?"

She heard his hesitant, hopeful tone, shook her head and pulled him closer. For some strange reason, her throat felt closed, and she couldn't speak. Couldn't tell him how wonderful he felt inside her, now the one fleeting moment of pain had fled.

Soon that glorious feeling rushed through her body again and she gasped, even as John found his own release. As they lay in each other's arms, within moments, they fell asleep.

Grace woke the following morning with John lying lightly atop her, kissing every curve and hollow of her body. Gasping in agony and delight at his touch, she relaxed when John proceeded to make thorough love to her again.

Afterward, they rode in the rental carriage to town for breakfast. John had rented the carriage for three days since he'd managed to talk Professor LaFoy into allowing him to begin work on Wednesday.

Grace's cheeks burned in embarrassment when LaFoy said of course he could begin later since the newlyweds needed to get to know each other better.

After breakfast, they spent the day walking the streets of Bozeman, shopping for dresses for Grace John insisted on purchasing since she'd need women's clothing. All of her clothes, other than her one traveling dress and the gown Margaret LaFoy had purchased for her, and of course, her wedding gown, were men's clothing.

John informed her never again did he want to see her wearing those. Shopping was the furthest thing from Grace's mind, though, and she simply enjoyed walking arm in arm with her husband along the walkways. Still, Grace sighed when John pulled her into a woman's shop and ended up choosing three dresses for her, undergarments, stockings and a pair of gloves. She didn't need shoes since Mrs. LaFoy had insisted on purchasing for her a pair of white satin heels to go with her wedding gown, and then a pair of lace-up leather oxfords, with a lower heel which were, by far, the best shoes Grace had ever owned. She owed the LaFoys' much she mused happily.

Every evening after supper, they walked, oblivious to their surroundings, enthralled with each other over the next few days. Grace found herself growing ever closer to her husband.

Soon John started working at the college. And while he worked during the day, she kept his apartment clean, and started writing a new penny dreadful. Each evening they went out for supper until after almost two weeks, Grace said she could cook. The small apartment had a two-burner coal-burning oven that worked well and a surprisingly good-sized ice box. There was no reason she couldn't go shopping and make food.

But often she found herself daydreaming about John, in particular his lovemaking. Lord, but the man knew how to love a woman. And she was so weak where he was concerned. A month, she'd told herself, they'd have one month together.

eight

The month passed quickly and, with each day drawing near the month's end, she loathed the very idea of leaving, though she'd sent a telegram and money to her aunt in Georgia to purchase tickets to San Francisco a few weeks before.

Soon, the last day arrived. She'd purchased her coach and train ticket to San Francisco, packed her trunks, and now they waited by the front door. John would fetch the coach for her once he arrived home from work, though she knew he'd try and talk her out of leaving. They'd talked the evening before, but he hadn't been able to change her mind.

While she wanted nothing better than to stay, she had a duty to her aunt and brother.

She was surprised when John seemed resigned to her

leaving and didn't put up a fight about it. Grace was disappointed and angry; did she mean so little to him after all? As the evening grew nearer to retiring, Grace was near tears. He'd been aloof, speaking little, choosing to sit on the divan and read one of his latest farm manuals while she tried to write—and failed.

Finally, she tossed down her pen and rose to her feet. "Have you no words for me, husband?"

John looked up at her, startled. "Sorry, I've been reading. Did I miss some important question from you, sweetheart?"

She sniffed at the endearment and cursed the tears forming in her eyes. "I'm leaving tomorrow, you know, and nothing you say or do will stop me."

He sighed and laid his manual down beside him. "I know."

His voice was quiet, resigned, and then Grace caught the loving look in his eyes and ran across the room and into his arms. She sat on his lap as he kissed her passionately, knowing well it would be the last time. Then, without a word, he came to his feet with her in his arms and made his way to the bedroom.

Undressing her reverently, his eyes settled on every curve of her body as he revealed it. She kept her eyes trained on him, biting her lip, her arms to her sides as she lay on her back, knowing this is what he needed. What he expected. He lay upon her then and took her for the last time as tears slipped from her eyes.

With no words the following morning, John loaded up the coach that had arrived for Grace. He rode with her to the station, his arm around her, her head of silky hair on his shoulder. He thought how she'd changed since he first met her from the prickly woman who dared to dress as a man and play a man's game to the sweet, pretty, utterly feminine woman in his arms. He thought how he'd changed from a single young man intent on his career to a man in love with a woman for the first time in his life and knew he couldn't give her up. She was a part of him as he was a part of her.

Then horror struck him; what if she was with child!

As the coach came to a halt, he turned to her and took her hands in his. "I want you to promise me that if you find you are with child, you'll contact me."

He was surprised when she nodded, guessing from the worrisome look on her face her thoughts had settled on the same thing.

"I will. I promise."

John opened the coach door and jumped down to the ground. Turning, he assisted her from the coach, taking in her peach-colored silk gown, the matching reticule in her hand. Her auburn hair she wore swept up in a chignon, revealing the delicate curve of her neck. Impetuously, uncaring of people strolling by, he pulled her into his arms and kissed her.

Finally, when he set her down on her feet, he looked up, startled at the sound of clapping. People, some he knew, some strangers, were smiling and watching them, enjoying the amorous moment between them. He grinned in return, tipped his hat and strolled into the train station with Grace. She kept her eyes downcast, her complexion pinkened with embarrassment.

"Oh, good grief, John. Everyone saw you kissing me."

He shrugged nonchalantly. "We're married, and most of them know it. Better we were kissing than fighting, don't you think?"

She gave him a dimpled smile. "True." She laughed then and looked away toward one long bench against a wall and gasped.

John saw the stricken look on her face and followed her gaze. An adolescent boy, his head lolling on his chest, sat on the bench, arms crossed over his chest. Beside him was an older woman in a bonnet, silk streamers tied in a perfect bow, who appeared to be just waking.

"Robbie? Aunt Lucinda?" Grace whispered as she slowly moved toward them.

Grace was shocked to see her family. They appeared exhausted, her brother sound asleep and her aunt just rousing.

She rushed the rest of the distance just as her aunt opened her eyes. "Grace?"

"Yes, it's me," Grace said, dropping to her knees beside her aunt.

Aunt Lucinda clamped her sturdy arms around Grace and squeezed her, even as tears squeezed from her eyes. "Oh, I didn't know when we'd ever find you—when we'd ever catch up with you!"

"You were following me?" Grace said, her eyes widening. "For how long? And did you receive any of my letters?"

"How could we, my girl, when we were following you?"

"Oh, Auntie, why didn't you stay put in Georgia? And where in the world did you get the money for the journey?"

"We'll discuss that later."

Robbie woke up and jumped to his feet. Hugging Grace around the waist, he hollered in her ear, "Dang, Sis, yer a sight for sore eyes! And sore legs and feet."

She pulled back from him and swept a lock of dark

brown hair off his forehead. "Now, why would your legs and feet be sore?"

"Cause we walked a fair bit along the journey to find you, that's why."

"What!"

"Shush, Robbie! Didn't I tell you we'd ease into telling her about our little adventure?"

"You mean little mishaps, don't you, Auntie?" the boy asked, grinning.

Rolling her eyes, Grace said, "Heaven help me. What did you two do?"

"How about we take them back to my place, Grace?"

She turned to John, having forgotten he stood right behind her.

"Who's he?" a suspicious Robbie asked.

"My—my..."

"Husband," John supplied.

"Husband?" Aunt Lucinda and Robbie shouted.

"You got yerself hitched when you was supposed to be earning money to send for us?" Aunt Lucinda asked.

"I have been earning money, and I wired it to you in Georgia just a few weeks ago. And now someone else will likely lift that money," Grace groaned.

"Well, if you weren't so fast movin' from town to town, we would have caught up with you sooner, wouldn't we have, Auntie?" Robbie asked.

"The boy's got a point. Why did you spend so little time in each town?" Lucinda said.

"Because each time I gambled and won it behooved me to get out of town—fast—if you know what I mean."

John said, "You mean you gambled your entire way across the country?"

"Of course."

"Why didn't you tell me? I assumed you'd run out of money and had been playing in just the last few locations until you reached Bozeman."

"Heck, no. Sis's been gambling for years, even fer our pa when he had a bad streak." Robbie grinned and added, "Grace never has a bad streak—only good ones."

John took Grace by the forearms and sternly stared at her. "No! More! Gambling! Understand?"

Grace's chin came up. "I'm the one to make that decision, not you, or anyone else."

"I'm your husband, and you promised to obey me."

"No, I didn't. I promised in sickness and in health to be true to you."

"I heard you say it."

She raised her brows. "I don't recall saying those words precisely."

"You said 'I do' after the priest said them, which is the same as saying them. You agreed."

"Oh, for heaven's sake. Every bride says, 'I do.' I was just going through the motions to help you, remember?"

"Yes, after I helped you. Remember?"

Aunt Lucinda stepped in. "Um, people are staring at you two arguing. I think we'd better leave."

"Yes, we'll talk more at home," John warned.

"You'll only need to put up with us for a night."

John scowled. "You are my wife, Grace, and you'll put up with me for the rest of your life."

"Are you threatening me?" she asked, her eyes widening.

"Yes."

He took her arm and hauled her out of the station as Robbie and Aunt Lucinda followed behind.

"Let go of my arm," Grace snapped.

John did, reluctantly, and walked away from her. Upon reaching a vacant coach headed for town, he paid for their ride and asked the coachman to load up the luggage.

Inside the coach, Grace and Aunt Lucinda sank down onto the seats, side by side, while Robbie took the seat opposite them. John sat down beside the boy who moved over and hugged the corner.

John frowned. *The boy treats me like the enemy. Aren't I the one to 'save the day?'*

At his apartment, after his houseguests freshened up, he conducted a meeting, calling on his talents as a natural-born teacher. He soon learned that shortly after Grace left Georgia, her brother and aunt followed her. But they lagged further and further behind, one misfortune after another struck. They'd been robbed, threatened, escaped being tossed into jail for Robbie being caught cheating at cards. All in all, they'd had quite an adventure.

Grace was livid and only settled down after she'd had more than her say. Her brother and aunt sat and took the chastisement until Grace settled down.

Throwing her hands up in the air, Grace said, "Well, now that I've sent every penny I'd earned for your travels, which has likely ended up in some lucky fellow's pocket, what shall we do?"

"Stay here. With me."

All three pairs of eyes stared at John.

"John," Grace began, "we can't possibly all stay here with you."

"We have a house."

"We do?" Grace asked.

"I hadn't told you yet, but President LaFoy gave us a wedding gift. The first home he and his wife lived in, located on the edge of town."

"You mean that Victorian monstrosity that requires so much work?" Grace asked, her face filled with dread.

John paced away from her, but not before Grace saw the pain in his eyes. She'd hurt him with her callous reply when all he'd been doing was trying to make a home for them.

Grace gently added, "I'm sure with a bit of care, the house will be beautiful."

He didn't turn to her, but continued to stare out the parlor window, his broad shoulders taut.

All the while she'd been arguing with John and her brother and aunt, she'd been thinking how she didn't want to leave Bozeman—or her husband. She had a feeling her relatives would be disappointed, but her aunt removed those worries with her next words.

"You know, from the little I've seen of this town, I like it."

"Me, too," Robbie said. "It'd be like livin' in the old west, you know? Grace? Uh, any chance I could have a horse?"

John looked at Robbie. "You must have a horse if you live here, boy."

"Can't we stay, Grace?"

"I don't know..."

"Please," John said, turning to face Grace. "Make me the happiest man alive. I won't let you leave...rather, I can't let you leave me. You're my wife."

Tears sparkled in Grace's eyes as she saw the sincerity on his face. "And you are my husband. But are you willing to put up with all of us?" she asked, her voice trembling.

John headed for her. Once he reached her, he swung her up in his arms. "I'd put up with a hundred more of your relatives to have you with me."

"Oh, no need to worry, my dear man," Aunt Lucinda said. "There are only the three of us left."

Amen, John mused. Ducking down, he found his wife's sweet lips and kissed her long and hard. He'd tamed the gambler and won a wife.

How lucky could a man get?

Don't miss out on your next favorite book!
Join the Satin Romance mailing list
www.satinromance.com/mail.html

~

THANK YOU FOR READING

~

Did you enjoy this book?

We invite you to leave a review at your favorite book site, such as Goodreads, Amazon, Barnes & Noble, etc.

DID YOU KNOW THAT LEAVING A REVIEW...

- Helps other readers find books they may enjoy.
- Gives you a chance to let your voice be heard.
- Gives authors recognition for their hard work.
- Doesn't have to be long. A sentence or two about why you liked the book will do.

about the author

Nancy Schumacher is the owner-publisher of Melange Books, LLC, writing under the pseudonyms, Nancy Pirri and Natasha Perry.

She is a member of Romance Writers of America. She is also one of the founders of the RWA chapter, Northern Lights Writers (NLW), in Minnesota.

www.nancypirri.com

 facebook.com/NancyPirriAuthor

also by nancy pirri

Montana Women

Katie and the Marshal

Annie and the Outlaw

Janie and the Judge

Laura and the Railroad Baron

The Montana Women Boxset (Books 1-4)

Contemporary Romance

Bait Shop Blue

All I Ever Wanted

I Wish You Love, a Spicy Romance Anthology

Make Me Behave (An Anthology) with Tara Fox Hall

Western Romance

Rugged Edges

Historical Romance

The MacAulay Bride

The Duke and the Lady Sleuth

A Husband For Christmas

Featured in the following anthologies:

Western Ways

Food and Romance Go Together, Vol. 2

Writing erotica as Natasha Perry

Ruined Hearts

Maid of His Heart